HAT   NEW HAT

by
Stan
and Jan
Berenstain

A Bright & Early Book

RANDOM HOUSE/ NEW YORK

Published in the United States by Random House Children's Books,
a division of Random House, Inc., New York.
Originally published by
Random House Children's Books, New York, in 1970.

Random House and the colophon and Bright & Early Books and
the colophon are registered trademarks of Random House, Inc.

Visit us on the Web!
randomhouse.com/kids
BerenstainBears.com

Educators and librarians, for a variety of teaching tools, visit us at
RHTeachersLibrarians.com

Library of Congress Cataloging-in-Publication Data
Berenstain, Stanley. Old hat, new hat,
by Stan and Jan Berenstain.
New York, Random House [1970] [29] p. col. illus. 24cm.
(A Bright & early book, BE9)
Summary: Can the perfect old hat really be replaced by a new one?
[1. Hats—Fiction. 2. Bears—Fiction. 3. Stories in rhyme.]
I. Berenstain, Janice, joint author.
II. Title. PZ8.3.B4493Ol [E] 77-117539
ISBN 978-0-394-80669-3 (trade)
ISBN 978-0-394-90669-0 (lib. bdg.)

Printed in the United States of America

68 67 66 65 64 63 62 61 60 59 58 57

Old hat.

Old hat.

New hat.

New hat

New hat

New hat

New hat

Too big.

Too small.

Too flat.

Too tall.

Too loose.

Too tight.

Too heavy.

Too light.

Too red.   Too dotty.

Too blue. Too spotty.

Too fancy.

Too frilly.

Too shiny.

Too silly.

Too
beady.

Too
bumpy.

Too
leafy.

Too
lumpy.

Too
feathery.

Too
scratchy.

Too
crooked.

Too
straight.

Too
pointed . . .

WAIT!

Just right!

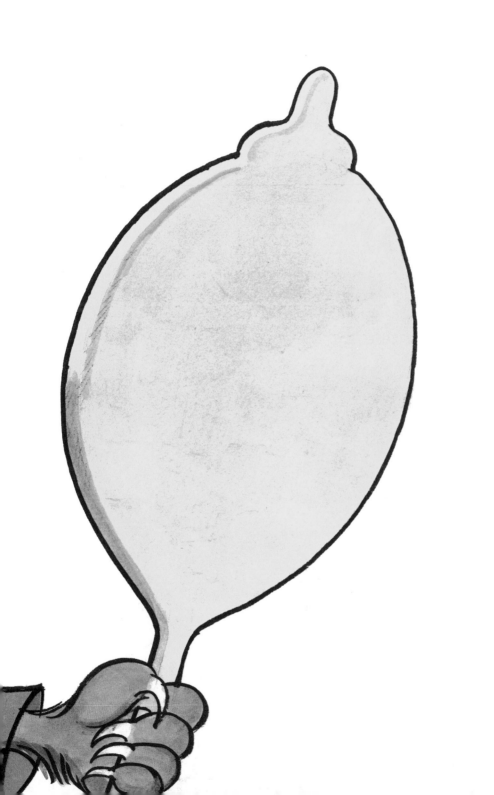

New hat.